For my beloved beachcomber, Bob
—J. S.

For all my teachers in Ames, Iowa—
with thanks for inspiring me along the way
—D. A.

SIMON & SCHUSTER BOOKS FOR YOUNG READERS • An imprint of Simon & Schuster Children's Publishing Division • 1230 Avenue of the Americas, New York, New York 10020 • Text copyright © 2009 by Judy Sierra • Illustrations copyright © 2009 by Derek Anderson • All rights reserved, including the right of reproduction in whole or in part in any form. • SIMON & SCHUSTER BOOKS FOR YOUNG READERS is a trademark of Simon & Schuster, Inc. • Book design by Chloë Foglia • The text for this book is set in Golden Cockerel. • The illustrations for this book are rendered in acrylic paint. • Manufactured in China • 10 9 8 7 6 5 4 3 2 1

LIBRARY OF CONGRESS CATALOGING-IN-PUBLICATION DATA • Sierra, Judy. • Ballyhoo Bay / by Judy Sierra; illustrated by Derek Anderson. — 1st ed. • p. cm • "A Paula Wiseman Book." • Summary: Mira Bella mobilizes her art students, from grandmothers to children, crabs to seagulls, to stop a dastardly plan for turning the beach at Ballyhoo Bay into an exclusive resort, and offers an alternative—leave the beach as it is. • ISBN-13: 978-1-4169-5888-8 (hardcover : alk. paper) • ISBN-10: 1-4169-5888-6 (hardcover : alk. paper) • [1. Stories in rhyme. 2. Social action—Fiction. 3. Beaches—Fiction. 4. Marine animals—Fiction. 5. Environmental protection—Fiction. 6. Artists—Fiction.] I. Anderson, Derek, 1969- ill. II. Title. • PZ8.3.S577Sav 2009 • [E]—dc22 • 2007049720

BALLYHOO BAY

By **Judy Sierra**

Illustrated by **Derek Anderson**

A Paula Wiseman Book
Simon & Schuster Books for Young Readers
New York   London   Toronto   Sydney

Every Saturday morning on Ballyhoo Beach,
Mira Bella, the artist, had classes to teach.

She taught etching and sketching
to grannies and kids,

and undersea sculpture to
swordfish and squids.

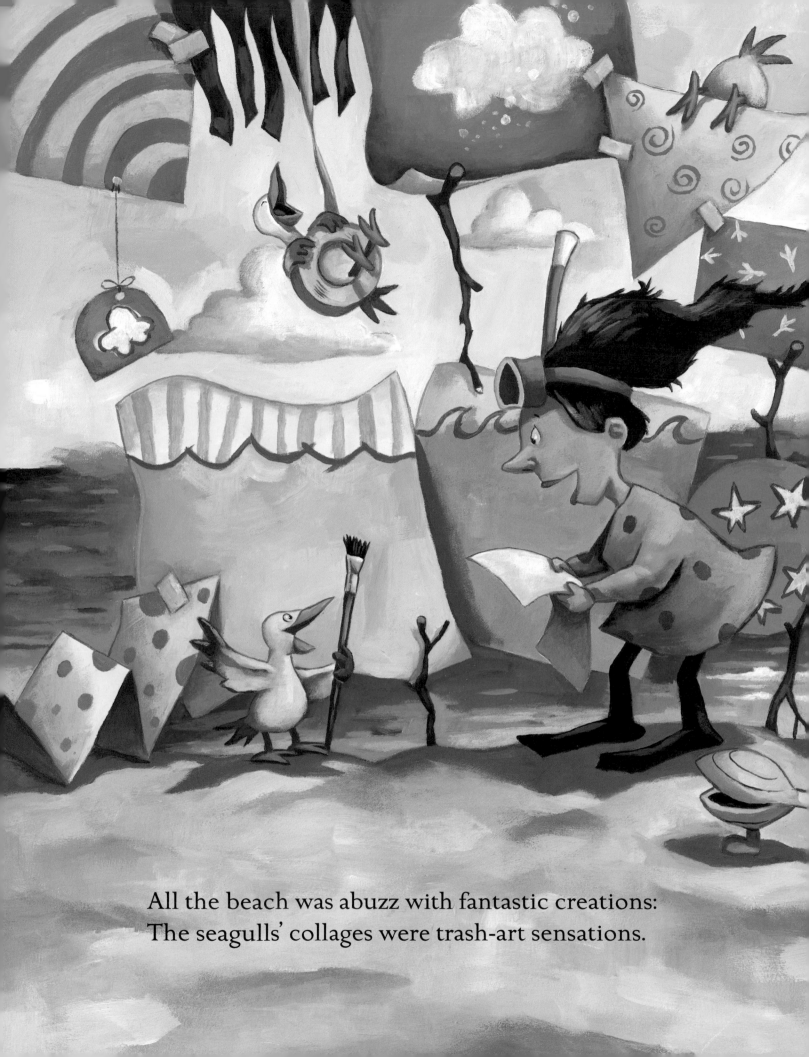

All the beach was abuzz with fantastic creations:
The seagulls' collages were trash-art sensations.

Pelicans painted,

crabs dabbled in clay,

and seals made mobiles
out of papier-mâché.

Otters drew silly self-portraits with pencils,
and sea squirts dyed T-shirts by spitting on stencils.

Mira Bella was planning a special event:
On the first day of June, in an elegant tent,
the Ballyhoo Art Fair was going to take place,
along with the Recycled Art-Cycle Race
(for creatures with feathers and flippers and fins,
where everyone enters and everyone wins).

But the last day of May dawned gloomy and gray.
Chilly winds whipped the waters of Ballyhoo Bay,
and bales of barbed wire appeared on the sand,
with a signpost announcing a dastardly plan.

Then a great wave of sorrow swept over the crowd.
Not one of them dared speak their feelings aloud.

Clams shut their shells, seagulls folded their wings,
and they all headed homeward to pack up their things.

Mira Bella cried, "Nonsense! We won't move away.
This ridiculous notion is only Plan A.
Let's create a Plan B and save Ballyhoo Bay."

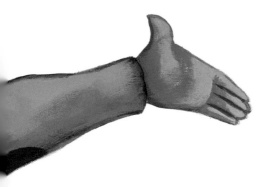

They rolled out the elegant tent and unzipped it.
Mira Bella drew lines, and the hermit crabs snipped it,
and everyone painted the places they loved—

the sea

and the sand

and the sky up above.

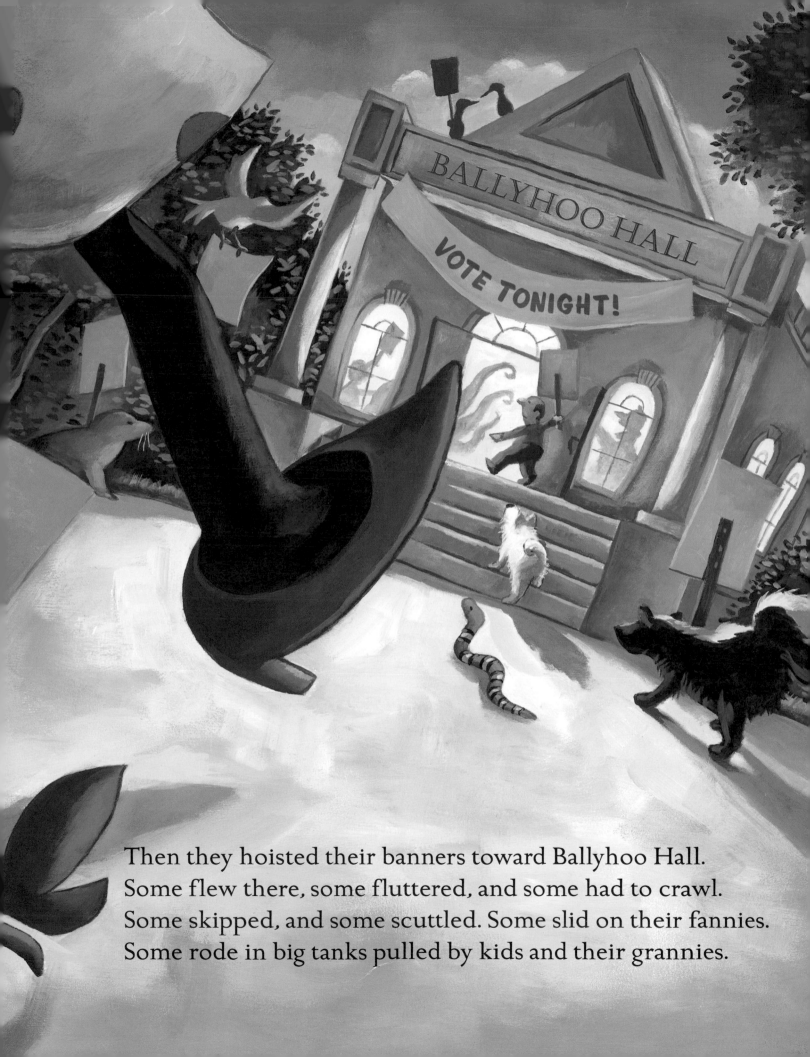

Then they hoisted their banners toward Ballyhoo Hall.
Some flew there, some fluttered, and some had to crawl.
Some skipped, and some scuttled. Some slid on their fannies.
Some rode in big tanks pulled by kids and their grannies.

The builders were flustered. They gasped, "How absurd!
A child cannot vote, or a fish or a bird!
We will never allow this to happen," they sputtered.
The town council huddled. They murmured. They muttered.

The kids, in a chorus, cried, "Look at Plan B,
Which is friendly and fun and fantastic and free.
It's an idea so simple you'll all shout, 'Gee whiz!
Why don't we leave the beach just as it is?'"

Then the grannies declared, "We think that Ballyhoo Bay
is for everyone, not just for those who can pay.
Now, whose heart is so shriveled they'd vote for Plan A?"

"Ahem," coughed the mayor. "The council will note that Plan A does not seem to get even one vote. Sooo, who votes for Plan B?"

Upward shot every paw,
every tentacle, hand, wing, antenna, and claw.
Even the builder guys had to say yes.

So they drove to the beach and they cleaned up their mess,
and the art fair next day was a smashing success.

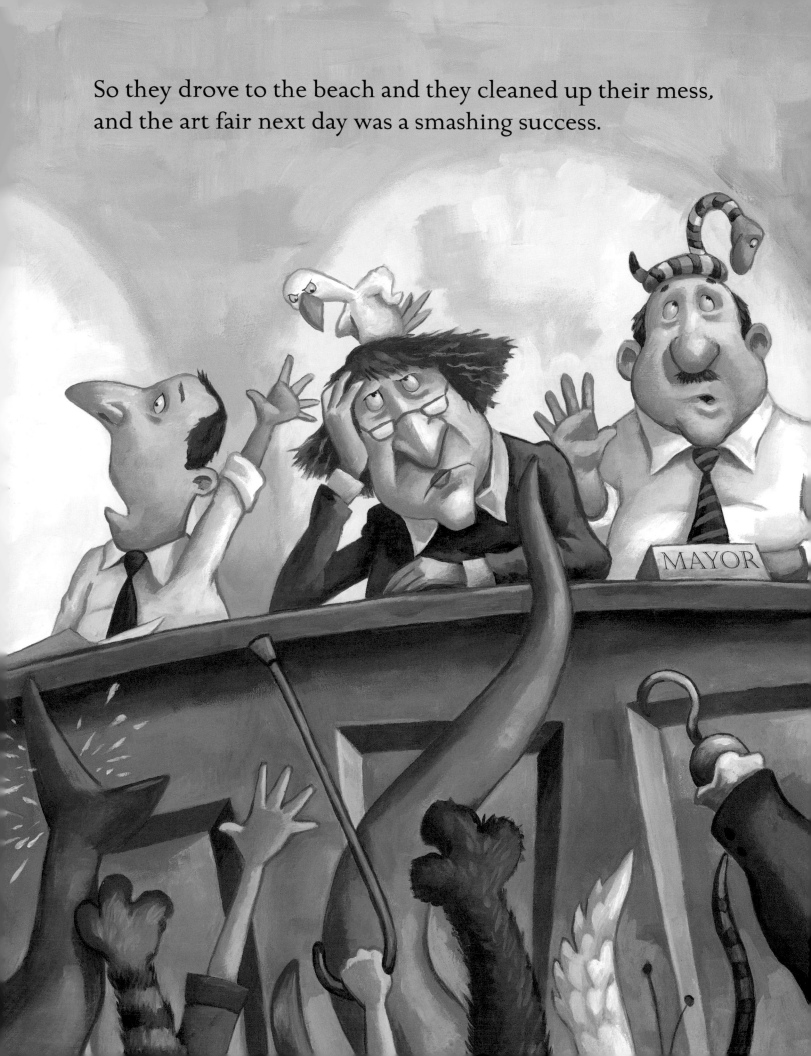

There was wet art and dry art
and high-in-the-sky art,

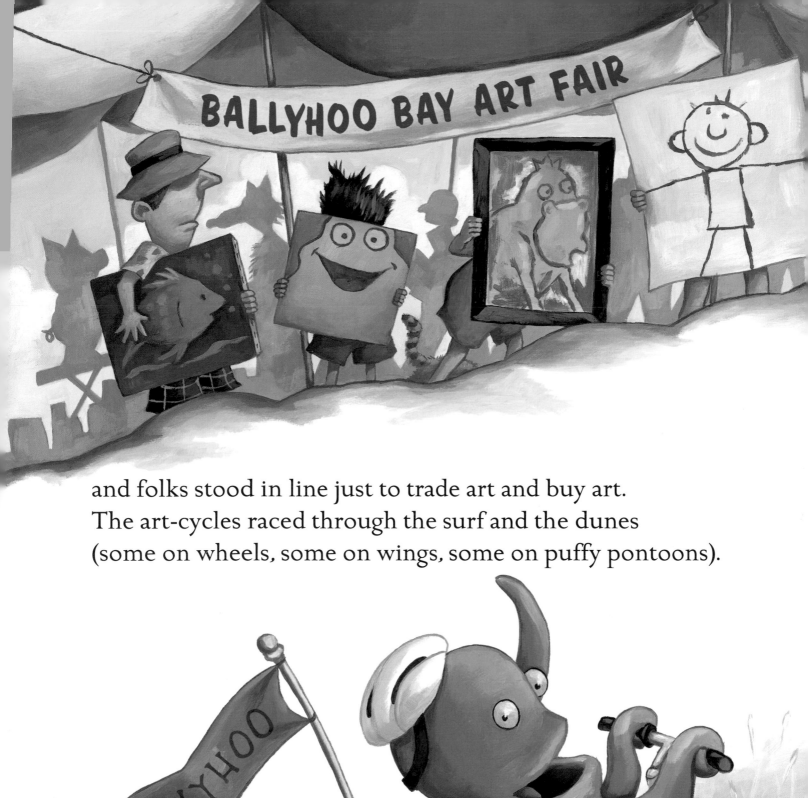

and folks stood in line just to trade art and buy art.
The art-cycles raced through the surf and the dunes
(some on wheels, some on wings, some on puffy pontoons).

Otters drew everyone's
portraits as prizes,

and sea squirts sold T-shirts in all shapes and sizes.

Mira Bella gazed out through the surf and the spray
as the sun set, resplendent, on Ballyhoo Bay.
"Truth is beauty," she said, "and they both saved the day."